I WENT TRICK-OR-TREATING

Paul Howard

BLOOMSBURY
CHILDREN'S BOOKS

LONDON   OXFORD   NEW YORK   NEW DELHI   SYDNEY

To my lovely
daughter, Bea

BLOOMSBURY CHILDREN'S BOOKS
Bloomsbury Publishing Plc
50 Bedford Square, London, WC1B 3DP, UK

BLOOMSBURY, BLOOMSBURY CHILDREN'S BOOKS and the Diana logo are trademarks of Bloomsbury Publishing Plc

First published in Great Britain 2018 by Bloomsbury Publishing Plc

Text and illustration copyright © Paul Howard 2018

Paul Howard has asserted his rights under the Copyright, Design and Patents Act, 1988,
to be identified as the Author and Illustrator of this work.

A catalogue record for this book is available from the British Library

ISBN: HB: 978 1 4088 9287 9; PB: 978 1 4088 9288 6; eBook: 978 1 4088 9286 2

2 4 6 8 10 9 7 5 3 1

Printed and bound in China by Leo Paper Products, Heshan, Guangdong

All papers used by Bloomsbury Publishing Plc are natural, recyclable products from
wood grown in well managed forests. The manufacturing processes conform to
the environmental regulations of the country of origin

To find out more about our authors and books visit www.bloomsbury.com and sign up for our newsletters

I went
Trick-or-Treating
and I scared...

Well... I went Trick-or-Treating
and I scared a
creepy, sleepy spider
and...

a naughty, warty toad!

I went Trick-or-Treating
and I scared a
creepy, sleepy spider,
a naughty,
warty toad
and...

Well, I went
Trick-or-Treating
and I scared
a creepy, sleepy spider,
a naughty, warty toad,
a wizard's noisy owl
and...

a sliding, gliding ghost!

I went Trick-or-Treating and
I scared a creepy, sleepy spider,
a naughty, warty toad,
a wizard's noisy owl,
a sliding, gliding ghost and...

some super

silly skeletons.

Well, I went
Trick-or-Treating and I
scared a creepy, sleepy spider,
a naughty, warty toad,
a wizard's noisy owl,
a **sliding, gliding ghost,**
some super silly skeletons
and...

a howling,
growling
AROooo! wolf.

I went Trick-or-Treating and
I scared a creepy, sleepy spider,
a naughty, warty toad,
a wizard's noisy owl,
a sliding, gliding ghost,
some super silly skeletons,
a howling, growling
wolf and...

a *spooky ship* of pirates!

I went
Trick-or-Treating
and I scared a
creepy, sleepy spider,
a naughty, warty toad,
a wizard's noisy owl,
a sliding, gliding ghost,
some super silly skeletons,
a howling, growling wolf,
a *spooky ship of pirates*
and...

a monster

boogie king.

I went Trick-or-Treating and
I scared a creepy, sleepy spider,
a naughty, warty toad,
a wizard's noisy owl,
a sliding, gliding ghost,
some super silly skeletons,
a howling, growling wolf,
a spooky ship of pirates,
a monster boogie king
and...

ten snazzy witch's cats

(and a pack of spooky-wooky flying bats!).

I went Trick-or-Treating and I scared

a creepy, sleepy spider,

a naughty, warty toad,

a wizard's noisy owl,

a sliding, gliding ghost.

some super silly skeletons,

a spooky ship
of pirates,

a howling,
growling wolf,

a monster
boogie king,

ten snazzy witch's cats
(and a pack of spooky-wooky flying bats!)

and that is everything.

Er – no it isn't.
You've forgotten
someone.

a creepy,
sleepy spider,

a naughty,
warty toad,

some super

Have I?
Who?

a spooky ship
of pirates,

a wizard's noisy owl,

a sliding, gliding ghost,

silly skeletons,

a howling, growling wolf,

a monster boogie king,

ten snazzy witch's cats
(and a pack of spooky-wooky flying bats!).

WAAAAAAA!

Mwa-Ha-Ha-Ha-Ha-Ha-Ha-Hee-Hee-Hee-Hee-Hee!

Happy Halloween,
everybody!